Sanju and Buddy

Sanmitha Veerakannan

Ukiyoto Publishing

All global publishing rights are held by

Ukiyoto Publishing

Published in 2023

Content Copyright © Sanmitha Veerakannan

ISBN 9789360165185

All rights reserved.
No part of this publication may be reproduced, transmitted, or stored in a retrieval system, in any form by any means, electronic, mechanical, photocopying, recording or otherwise, without the prior permission of the publisher.

The moral rights of the author have been asserted.

This is a work of fiction. Names, characters, businesses, places, events, locales, and incidents are either the products of the author's imagination or used in a fictitious manner. Any resemblance to actual persons, living or dead, or actual events is purely coincidental.

This book is sold subject to the condition that it shall not by way of trade or otherwise, be lent, resold, hired out or otherwise circulated, without the publisher's prior consent, in any form of binding or cover other than that in which it is published.

This title is produced in Association with Pachyderm Tales

www.pachydermtales.com

ACKNOWLEDGEMENT

I whole heartedly thank,

Mohanasundari Jaganathan,

(Managing Director of Sharp Electrodes Pvt Ltd)

for funding this project.

Without her, this book would not be possible!

This book was a part of workshop conducted in our college, NGM College Pollachi and Pachyderm Tales.

I whole heartedly thank our management, our teachers and HOD of English Dept, NGM as well as Suja Mam for this initiative.

Thanks to my friend to support and help me to complete my work.

I am a golden fish. God has granted me a boon which is to look like a doll.

My name is Buddy. Two people brought me at a sea fair and took me home. They placed me inside a big fish tank filled with water.

I felt so lonely as I had no company inside the tank.

The family consists of a father, mother, and their only daughter. The little girl is short and has long curly hair with a dusky skin.

Her parents spend most of their time, working. They leave for work early in the morning, leaving her alone in the huge mansion.

She has lots of toys to play with. But still, she was lonely like me. She used to write and draw all the time. I wanted to know more about her.

One day, the girl started crying all of a sudden. She came near my tank and started narrating her story to me, sobbing.

"I am Sanju" She introduced herself. "I feel like I am always alone in this big house. My parents never consider my existence here. They are just concerned about their work and business. They leave the house early in the morning and returns late at night. By that time, I would have been fast asleep."

"I have nobody to talk to and play with. All I have is a bunch of lifeless toys and some pencils and books. My parents do not love me. I am a burden to them." She cried out loud as she finished her narration.

Hearing all this, I felt my mouth moving and I was talking to her.

The girl was surprised and asked "Can a fish speak? How could you speak human language? Where did you learn it from?" I smiled and decided to tell her my story.

"Hello Sanju. My name is Buddy. I was born in the sea to a big family of golden fish. I was enjoying my life with my clan. All of a sudden, I was caught on a net by a fisherman and was taken to a pet shop. I was enclosed inside a large fish tank along with many other little fishes. I was slowly adapting my life at the new habitat."

"But then, I was again uprooted from there when your parents bought me. But now, I feel a bit even more lonely. My greatest wish is to get out from here and be with my family once again. I have a super power too. I could grant one wish for anyone who helps me to get back to my family." I explained.

We got to know each other so well and Sanju started writing and reciting little rhymes for me.

Sanju and Buddy

'Buddy Buddy come with me

I will take you to the sea.

Try to speak some words with me.

Let me watch the sleeping sea,

Come and play some games with me.

Chance of life is like a sea.'

After we had spent a lot of time

together, Sanju was ready to take me back to the sea. She took me in to the sea in a small bowl filled with water.

As we reached the sea shore, we looked at each other in a hope to meet again.

"Tell me your wish

Sanju. I will make it happen for you."

I reminded her of the boon.

"I need a friend named Buddy. I want her to be my greatest friend and companion all along my life. She should not leave me at any cost." She spoke.

"As you wish little girl."

I said, thanking her for all the help that she had done for me.

She dropped me inside the crystal blue waters of the sea. I swam back to my parents and siblings, starting my lost life with them again.

As Sanju reached back to her home thinking of Buddy, she saw her neighbour's daughter sitting there, waiting for her. Her name was Buddy too.

Sanju couldn't believe her eyes as Buddy's boon had come true. She was so excited and started playing with Buddy.

They became so close to each other and were best friends for the rest of their lives.

Sanju no longer felt lonely. Whenever she saw Buddy's face, she thanked the little fish...

The Author

Sanmitha Veerakannan is an under graduate student of English literature at NGM college. She is an aspiring writer and motivates herself to write for children. She does not believe in restricting oneself to a particular area of talent. She is not only a talented and creative writer but have mastered over other arts like bridal makeup, handicrafts, painting and many more. Her expertise over various fields of arts have gained her immense and strong support from her family, peers, and teachers.

www.ingramcontent.com/pod-product-compliance
Lightning Source LLC
LaVergne TN
LVHW041644070526
838199LV00053B/3552